T0199194

Avanier
and
the
Legend of the
Guardian Stone

WRITTEN AND ILLUSTRATED BY:

D. Lewis

AuthorHouse™
1663 Liberty Drive
Bloomington, IN 47403
www.authorhouse.com
Phone: 1 (800) 839-8640

This book is printed on acid-free paper.

ISBN: 978-1-7283-3055-6 (sc)
ISBN: 978-1-7283-3054-9 (hc)
ISBN: 978-1-7283-3056-3 (e)

Library of Congress Control Number: 2019915791

Print information available on the last page.

Published by AuthorHouse 10/07/2019

authorHOUSE

Avanier
and
the
Legend of the
Guardian Stone

Now on their way, Ava Bear has traveled far beyond, the Birchwood Forest. Mr. Balloon noticed it was getting very late, and the sun was starting to set very low in the sky.

Ava bear asked Mr. Balloon, can I tell you a secret? "It is my honor to keep it safe," replied Mr. Balloon. Ava Bear tells him, "I don't like the dark very much; it makes me very afraid." Mr. Balloon replied I have a secret as well. And at that moment, Mr. Balloon began to shine like sun rays bursting through the clouds!

Ava bear smiled ear to ear thinking whoa; my Noon glows in the dark! You see Ava, "Long ago, I was more than just a companion." I am the last of Glenmore, said Mr. Balloon. Glenmore? Ava asked.

Far to the west above the Aladorn Mountains, there is a city; it is the last of its kind. "It is where the stone has been kept for many generations said, Mr. Balloon.

I thought you were just a "Noon" that could talk, said Ava. Mr. Balloon laughed and said, I am a balloon and very much more. "Were you always a balloon?" asked Ava. For many years, I soared high above the trees, and protected the lands, replied Mr. Balloon.

How did you fly so high? Asked Ava. Before I used to have bronze wings that allowed me to go far above the clouds, replied Mr. Balloon. At night when I was scared, my daddy used to tell me a story about how we were all safe because the light shines even in the dark. Wait! You're a Guardian Eagle! Said Ava.

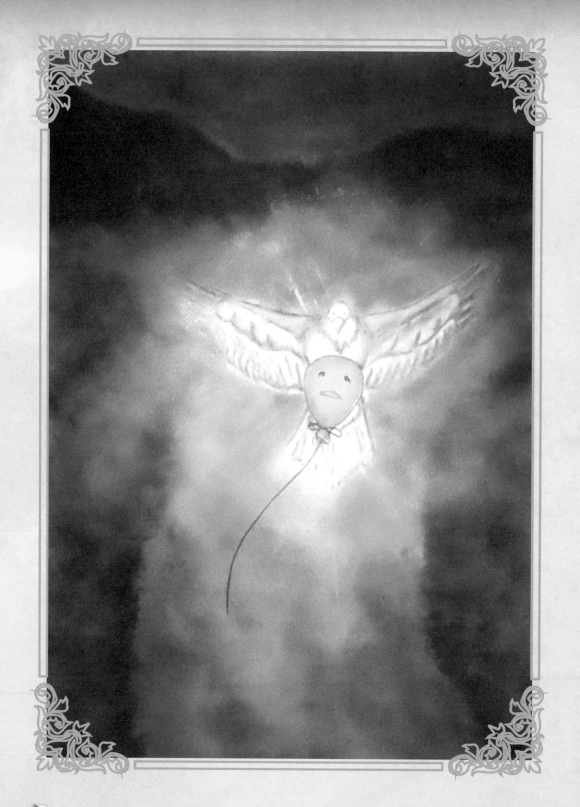

A long time ago, I used to be one, said Mr. Balloon. It's said that Guardian Eagles could only tell their name to someone that promises not to say it to anyone, said Ava. Mr. Balloon replied you had trusted me with your secret. I trust you with mine. My name is Wynmere, said, Mr. Balloon. "Can you still be my Noon?" asked Ava?

would be honored to be your "Noon," replied Wynmere. If you were a Guardian Eagle, why are you a balloon? Asked Ava. In the final days between the Eagles and the Torrack, the Guardian Stone concealed me in this form to hide my true identity. Torrack? Ava asked.

There was a time when the Guardians and the Torrack lived in harmony. The Eagles protected the skies while the Torrack, the people of Glenmore protected the lands. Doram seduced the Torrack; he turned them against the Eagles.

The Torrack cast out the eagles from Glenmore and hid the talisman, so the eagles could no longer fly. The Torrack were now left to rule the land and the sky. The two sides fought to have power over the stone for many years until only one of them each remained.

Seeing all that has been lost, the Guardian Stone called the last Eagle and the Torrack to the sacred forest, to restore balance once again. The eagle bowed and asked forgiveness for what has been done, in an attempt to claim the land once and for all. The Torrack struck the eagle cutting off one of his wings.

The Guardian Stone announced with the power of a storm, "Torrack, you have no forgiveness in your heart! In this form, you shall destroy all things, so no form shall you have. Embracing this knowledge that there cannot be light, without dark. In a crash of thunder, the Torrack was transformed into nothing more than a vile gust of wind, having no place to rest.

After a time, the vile winds found me; they meant to seek their revenge and took me away from the young prince. In this haste, not knowing it led me right to you Ava, said Wynmere. "I need to get you back to the sacred forest right away!" said Ava. It is not your time yet, and you are doing more than I can ask of you by taking me home, replied Wynmere.

Do you have any memories of your mother? Asked Wynmere. No Papa won't talk about her to me, he says he will tell me when I'm older, said Ava. I'm afraid time is running out, and I must tell you. Ava, you are the last heir to the throne of Glenmore, your real name is Avanier, and your mother was their queen, said Wynmere.

I'm not sure I understand, my mother was a queen? My Papa and I need to talk when I get home, Ava thought to herself. Your mother's name was Anadea. I always told Papa I was a princess, said Ava. Yes indeed, and now you are Glenmore's rightful queen, and I take the oath to stand as your Guardian, said Wynmere.

Wait! If I'm Glenmore's last queen, that makes me. Oh no! A Torrack! Said Ava. Not all Torrack betrayed the queen in the final days. Some fled, others drifted into memories, and some became legends, said Wynmere.

Wynmere," what happened to my mother?" asked Ava. The queen tried to undo the harm Doram did to the torrack people before she escaped, but greed and envy are all they saw. They said why should we be down here working the lands while the eagles flew around and watched? The Queen told the people the eagles are our allies; they see what we cannot.

It was too late though; the Torrack wanted to govern the land and skies alone. They wanted a new ruler, a stronger ruler, and they chose one, King Doram. By the time the Torrack learned of Doram's deceit many years had passed and the battles for Glenmore had already begun..

Why did the Guardian Stone turn you into a balloon? Asked Ava. The Eagle lying hurt was dying. The Guardian Stone shooting rays of gold light all through the forest; gave up the last of its power to save the eagle. Concealing him in this form you see before you.

What is the Guardian Stone? Asked Ava. It is the foundation where the balance of life was created. You see Ava the forest cannot live without air, and there would be no air without the forest; it is this balance that sustains life all around us, said Wynmere.

Can the stone help you, Wynmere? Will you be a guardian again, Asked Ava? If life returns to the forest, then there might be a way, said Wynmere.

I am sure Papa is worried about me by now, Ava said. I can help you, said Wynmere. There was a great snow owl nesting in the tree, just a little ahead of the road. Wynmere looked at the owl and started to glow a light blue like the morning sky. Shortly after the owl bowed his head, a flew off heading east.

What happened to the owl, did we scare him away? Asked Ava. No, I asked him to deliver an important message for me, said Wynmere. I'm going to return you to the sacred forest. I want you to fly again, said Ava. You have your mothers' spirit, and your father's honor replied Wynmere.

What message did you send? Asked Ava. I asked the great owl, to tell the prince of Glenmore that Avanier and the Last Guardian are on their way to restore life to the sacred Forest.

But that is another story.

Printed in the United States
By Bookmasters